DON'T GO IN THE CELLAR

BY JEREMY STRONG

illustrated by
Scoular Anderson

Librarian Reviewer
Laurie K. Holland
Media Specialist (National Board Certified), Edina, MN
MA in Elementary Education, Minnesota State University, Mankato, MN

Reading Consultant
Elizabeth Stedem
Educator/Consultant, Colorado Springs, CO
MA in Elementary Education, University of Denver, CO

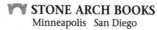 STONE ARCH BOOKS
Minneapolis   San Diego

First published in the United States in 2006
by Stone Arch Books, A Capstone Imprint
151 Good Counsel Drive, P.O. Box 669,
Mankato, Minnesota 56002.
www.capstonepub.com

Published by arrangement with
Barrington Stoke Ltd, Edinburgh.

Library of Congress Cataloging-in-Publication Data
Don't Go in the Cellar / by Jeremy Strong; illustrated by Scoular
Anderson.
    p. cm. — (Pathway Books)
    Summary: Following a foreboding clue, Zack and Laura search for
a cellar in Zack's new house and discover a "story machine" that causes
them a lot of trouble.
    ISBN-13: 978-1-59889-002-0 (library binding)
    ISBN-10: 1-59889-002-6 (library binding)
    ISBN-13: 978-1-59889-194-2 (paperback)
    ISBN-10: 1-59889-194-4 (paperback)
    [1. Adventure and adventurers—Fiction. 2. Storytelling—Fiction.]
I. Anderson, Scoular, ill. II. Title. III. Series.
PZ7.S92356Don 2006
[Fic]—dc22   2005026572

Cover Illustrator: Jeana Lidfor

Printed in the United States of America in Stevens Point, Wisconsin.
062010
005833R

TABLE OF CONTENTS

CHAPTER 1

THE WRITING ON THE WALL

"Why does Laura have to stay here?" asked Zack.

"Because her mom is my best friend, and I want to help her out. She has to go away for a few days," Zack's mom told him.

"But I don't like Laura."

"You don't have to like her. She's just like family."

Zack Dawson went up to his room and sat on his bed. Laura was coming to visit. There was no getting out of it. Zack did not like Laura. This was why:

1. She was a girl.

2. She was smart.

3. She had pushed him into the pool. (Okay, he was only six at the time. He got wet. Very wet. And Laura laughed at him.)

4. Laura had pushed Zack into the pool. So Zack had pushed her into the flower bed. Then Zack had a big laugh but not for long. Mom's best flowers got smashed.

Zack's mom had been very upset with him. She hadn't been upset with Laura. That was not fair. Laura had pushed him first. It was the first time that Zack saw how unfair life could be.

Now they were both 12, and Zack still didn't like Laura. He sat on his bed, feeling angry.

There was so much stress in Zack's life at the moment. His family had just moved into a new house. It was a long way from their old home. There was a new street and new faces next door.

There was also a new school, new teachers, a new town, a new job for Dad, and so on. Now, when they had been in the new house for only three days, Laura was coming to visit.

Zack gave a big sigh. He lay on his side and stared at the wall. It was a nice day and the sun was shining into his bedroom. In the bright light, Zack saw some words on the wall that he hadn't seen before.

The writing was low on the wall. The letters were very small and written in ink. They said:

DON'T GO IN THE CELLAR

That was all.

Zack sat up in bed. I've seen this message before, he thought.

His parents found an old wardrobe in his bedroom when they moved in. Zack had looked inside. There was nothing in it, but on the back of one of the doors some words had been cut into the wood:

DON'T GO IN THE CELLAR

The weird thing was, the new house didn't *have* a cellar.

DON'T GO IN THE CELLAR

CHAPTER 2

LAURA

"Laura's here!" Zack's mom called up to him. Zack already knew she was there. He had heard the taxi drive away and then the doorbell ring. He heard his mom talking to someone.

"Come down and say hello," Zack's mom called up the stairs. She smiled at Laura. "Zack's a bit shy," she said.

Up in his room, Zack heard what his mom said. His face turned red.

Why did parents always get these things wrong? Why did they do this to him? Zack shut his eyes and counted to ten. Then he went downstairs.

"Hi," said Laura. "I like your new house."

She smiled, and her face lit up. Zack said hello in a low voice.

"My, how you've grown!" said Zack's dad to Laura as he took her bag.

Why do parents always say that? Why do they bother? wondered Zack. Of course she's grown! That's what children do as they get older! We haven't seen her for six years!

Zack didn't say a thing. Zack walked slowly behind his dad as he showed Laura through the new house.

While she looked at the rooms, Zack looked at her. In fact, she has grown up, he thought. I didn't think she would be like this.

She was almost as tall as he was. Her hair was still black, but now it was so long she had to keep pushing it back to keep it out of her face. She smiled all the time.

Zack's dad showed Laura her room. "That's Zack's room over there," he said, "and you'll be in here."

Zack had an idea. "Show her the cellar, Dad," he said.

Mr. Dawson shook his head. "He keeps asking me that, Laura. And I keep telling him there isn't one. I think he's playing some kind of joke on me, but I don't think it's very funny."

Laura smiled and Zack felt angry. Mr. Dawson went down to the kitchen, and they were left alone.

"Why do you want to see the cellar?" asked Laura.

"Because there isn't one," Zack said.

"Do you always talk in riddles?" asked Laura.

For a moment Zack was silent. Should he show Laura the message on the wall? He felt he had to.

"Come and see something," he said, and they went to his room.

First he showed her the wardrobe. "This was the only thing in the room when we moved here," he said.

She read the words cut into the door.

"How do you know it means this house?" asked Laura. "It could have been written inside the wardrobe before it ended up here."

14

"I wondered about that myself,"
said Zack. "But I have something else
to show you," he said.

"What is it?" Laura asked.

"I want you to read something," added Zack. "You can only read it if you look closely at the wall."

Laura leaned down to read the message. Zack moved a lamp so that it shined on the words on the wall.

"*Don't go in the cellar*," read Laura. She sat up and looked at Zack. "Well," she began, "it must be under the house somewhere. How exciting! It's just like a Harry Potter story. Come on!"

Zack walked slowly behind her. He felt his life was being taken over.

CHAPTER 3

THE CELLAR

Zack and Laura looked for the cellar
for hours. Mrs. Dawson was amazed at
how well they were getting along.

"I think Zack really likes Laura,"
she told Mr. Dawson.

"How can you tell? He snaps at her
all the time," said her husband.

"That's what I mean," Mrs. Dawson
said. "Of course, Zack doesn't know he
likes her."

Mr. Dawson looked at her and shook his head. "Women are so odd," he said. He watched Zack and Laura walk past the window. "So if Zack likes her, does she like him?"

"Oh, yes! Laura's liked Zack since she was six! That's why she pushed him into the pool!" Mrs. Dawson told him.

Mr. Dawson shook his head again. "I will never understand women."

Luckily, Laura and Zack didn't know that Zack's parents were talking about them. They were too busy looking for the cellar. They had been all over the house, but so far, they hadn't found anything.

They went into the garden and tried to find a door to the cellar.

"It could be anywhere," said Zack.

"Not anywhere," said Laura. "It's got to be near the house. In fact, I bet it's right up against the house wall. What about in the greenhouse?"

"It's full of junk," said Zack.

"I know. Come on." Laura pushed her way into the greenhouse. It was very small and full of old boards and piles of pots.

"This is more of a dump than a greenhouse," said Zack.

Laura looked hard at the corner where the greenhouse joined one of the walls of the house. The corner was piled high with old junk.

"Help me move this stuff. It might be behind here," said Zack.

The big boards were hard to lift. Everything had to be moved around the greenhouse so that they could get near the corner.

"Well, well, well," said Zack.

There *was* an old door.

In fact, it was more like half a door. It only came up to their chests. But it was a door. Someone had painted a message on it in large red letters.

DON'T GO IN THE CELLAR

"I think we'd better go in," grinned Laura.

"Do you always do what you're told not to?" asked Zack.

"Of course," Laura said. She turned the knob and pushed hard at the door. She almost fell inside as it swung open. Zack had to grab her to keep her from falling down the dark steps on the other side. He pulled her back, and she fell against him.

"You're so strong," Laura said and gave him a sweet smile.

"Oh, shut up," said Zack, and he led the way down.

The smell was old and stale, but it wasn't a bad smell, just different. They were standing in a small room. There were cobwebs everywhere. A very large, dusty machine filled the space.

The machine had great big wheels with lots of cogs to make them turn. Huge metal rods and giant chains linked the wheels. There were levers for lifting things and pistons to move up and down.

At the far end of the room was a big metal chest. What could be inside? On one side was a large lever. On top of the chest was a dirty glass window, the size and shape of a mail slot.

Zack rubbed the window clean. It was blank.

"I don't know what this window is for," he said.

"How about this?" asked Laura, with her hand on the lever. "What does this do?"

"Don't touch it!" said Zack.

24

So Laura pulled the lever. She had
told Zack that she always did what she
was told not to do. The machine began
to creak and roar. The wheels turned.
The chains clanked. The floor began to
shake. There was a noisy CLUNK, and
a word came up in the dirty window.
Zack looked at it. It said:

HORROR

"What does that mean?" asked
Laura with a grin.

CHAPTER 4

HORROR

A moment later she found out.

A skeleton jumped on her back.

"Aaargh! Aaargh! Get it off me!" yelled Laura.

Zack grabbed a broom. He hit the clacking bones until they fell in a heap around Laura's feet. She stared down at the pile of bones in horror. Then all at once, the bones joined together and walked away, clicking as they went.

26

Laura's face was very pale.

"What's going on?" she asked in a whisper.

She looked around in panic. But
the cellar was silent and still. Two eyes
glowed in the dark. Then four eyes.
Six eyes. A hundred eyes! Laura clung
to Zack. Zack clung to Laura. "We're
being watched," she said. "Who are
they? What do they want?"

"Walk toward the steps, very
slowly," Zack said softly.

Voices began to whisper in the dark.

There seemed to be lots of voices. They chattered and licked their lips. "Zack? Laura? Come over here. We want to eat you. Oh yummy yum! Oh yes! An arm for me and a leg for you! Yum yum yum!"

Laura and Zack reached the bottom of the steps.

"Run for it!" yelled Zack, and he pushed Laura in front of him. They raced up the steps and almost fell into the sunshine. Zack looked around. It was all right. Everything was back to normal. No skeletons. No monsters. They were safe. Zack hoped Laura could not hear his heart thumping.

"You're a mess," he told her as he brushed the cobwebs from her hair.

She gazed back at him with big, wide eyes.

"You saved my life," she said.

Zack didn't know what to say.

"Zack? Laura? It's time for lunch!" Mrs. Dawson called from the house.

She sounded so normal. It was what they both needed to hear. They wanted to forget what had just happened.

"Come on, lunch is on the table," called Mrs. Dawson again from the kitchen.

"Don't say a word," Zack said to Laura as they went in.

"Your mom would just think we were making things up," she replied.

Zack sat at the table in a daze. He saved her life? He wasn't so sure. He didn't feel as if he'd saved her life. He felt confused — very confused.

"So how are you two getting along after all these years?" asked Mr. Dawson. Zack gave a shrug. Mr. Dawson winked at his wife. Zack saw the wink and sank into an angry silence.

"I've made a pie," said Zack's mom.

She opened the oven door, reached in and gave a yell. She yelled and she yelled and she yelled.

It was not a pie that came out of the oven. It was a huge, hairy spider as big as an octopus. Its giant legs clicked and clacked. It had very large jaws and seven huge, round eyes. One eye looked at Zack. One eye looked at Laura. One eye looked at Mrs. Dawson, and the other four stared at Mr. Dawson.

Mr. Dawson jumped up and slammed the oven door, shutting the spider inside. He turned up the heat. A weird howl came from inside the oven. There was a strong smell of sizzling hair.

Mrs. Dawson was shaking all over.

She pointed to the oven. She couldn't say a word. Her hair stood on end. Laura gripped Zack's hand under the table.

Zack gulped. "So, no pie then," he said, smiling. "How about pudding?"

Laura gazed around the room.

What was going to happen next? Laura wondered. "The walls!" she gasped. "Look at the walls!"

The kitchen walls seemed to be coming alive. They were moving and shaking as if something was about to burst through. Little holes appeared, like little dots, getting bigger and bigger. And out of the holes came —

Giant slugs — slugs as big as a man's arm!

Mr. Dawson ran to Mrs. Dawson and threw his arms around her. "What do we do?" they yelled.

"Quick!" cried Laura. She pulled at Zack and dragged him outside. "We must get back to the cellar and turn off that machine!"

CHAPTER 5

THE STORY MACHINE

They almost fell down the steps.

"Quick!" panted Laura. "Help me push the lever back to where it was!"

They grabbed the rusty lever and pushed as hard as they could, but there was no way they could get it to go back.

"It won't work!" cried Laura.

"We can't give up," Zack told her.

"Mom and Dad are being attacked by giant slugs!" Zack exclaimed. "Come on! Let's see if the lever will move the other way."

They pushed the lever once more. Slowly, it began to move.

CLUNK!

A new message flashed in the little window. Laura and Zack looked at it.

FAIRY TALE

Laura frowned and looked at Zack.

"Fairy tale?" she asked.

Zack took a quick look around the cellar. No skeletons. Phew! Things seemed to be back to normal, if only for a moment or two.

"I think I know what this is all about," Zack began slowly. "I think this is some kind of story machine. It makes different kinds of stories. The first kind was horror, and now it's —"

"— going to make a fairy tale," nodded Laura. "That explains why there's a dragon behind you."

Zack spun around only to see something small scuttle away behind the old table.

Zack smiled and relaxed. It was a dragon all right, but it was very small.

"Poor thing! It must be scared of us." Zack held out his hand to the little dragon. He picked it up.

Laura watched and held her breath.

How could Zack pick up the dragon? thought Laura. What if it tried to bite him? What if it could breathe fire? All at once her heart almost stopped.

What if the baby dragon's mother is just around the corner? she thought.

Just then there was a loud crash. Some bricks fell out of the wall, and a knight in shining armor came crashing into the room. He was waving a huge sword. The broad, blue blade gleamed as he swung it back and forth.

"All right, where's the dragon?" he boomed. "I know there's a dragon in here. I am Sir Knight-in-Shining-Armor, and this is my sword, Dragon-Cutter. It always glows blue like this when a dragon is near. I must slay it at once!"

"But it's just a baby," said Zack, holding the little dragon close.

The knight strode toward him. Zack felt the wind as the sword cut the air above his head.

"Babies grow up!" roared Sir Knight. "I am the dragon slayer! Hand it over at once!"

He stepped forward and held his sword high above his head. Zack shrank back. He knew that both he and the baby dragon were going to die.

Laura tried hard to think. What could she do? Then her face lit up. Yes! It might work!

She ran to the bottom of the steps and began to wail and moan and pull her hair.

The knight turned to her at once.

"What? A poor princess in distress? I must save her!"

He strode across to Laura and went down on one knee.

"Fair princess," he began, "what's the matter? Are you about to be eaten by wolves? Is a wicked wizard about to turn you into a frog? How can I help?"

"Oh, woe is me," said Laura, as if she was a poor princess.

She put her hand to her head and gave a groan. "There are huge slugs in the kitchen, and they are about to eat my friend's mom and dad! Only you can save them!"

Zack was amazed.

Hmmm, he thought, she's smart.

She's saving me and my parents at the same time, thought Zack. That's a clever trick!

"Do not fear!" cried Sir Knight-in-Shining-Armor. "I shall slay those slimy slugs, and we shall all live happily ever after!"

"You are my hero!" said Laura, with a sigh.

Zack didn't like *that* very much.

Sir Knight-in-Shining-Armor charged up the stairs, and Zack and Laura ran after him. Outside, they saw that something odd was going on.

There was a crowd of people around Zack's house, and they seemed to be eating it.

43

CHAPTER 6

FOOD FIGHT

The giant slugs were gone.

"Hmmm, this is good gingerbread," said one man as he munched away at one of the walls of the house.

What he said was true.

The walls were made of gingerbread. The roof was frosting. The door was made of chocolate.

People were eating the house!

Zack's parents were running back
and forth, trying to pull people away
from the house. They were very upset.

"Don't do that," they were saying. "This is our house! Stop eating our front door!"

All at once there was a loud crash and the garage caved in. One wall had been eaten away by the crowd.

"They're eating us out of house and home!" cried Mrs. Dawson. "I don't understand it. First we had a giant spider, then slugs, and now our house is being eaten as we stand here. And why is there a knight in shining armor clanking around the place? Oh, it's all too much!"

Zack and Laura looked at each other and nodded.

"Back to the cellar," said Zack. "How long is this going to go on?"

"Come on!" Laura exclaimed. "Or there'll be nothing left of your house."

Back in the cellar, they pushed the lever once more.

CLUNK!

"What does it say?" Zack asked. He was nervous.

SLAPSTICK

"What does that —" Laura began.

"Urffff!"

A custard pie came out of nowhere and hit Laura in the face. She wiped the custard from her eyes and gave Zack an angry look.

"Did you do that? I'll get you!" Laura rushed at him, slipped on a banana peel, and fell flat on her face.

Zack laughed. "Now that's funny!"

This made Laura even angrier.

She got up and ran toward Zack again. He turned to run. There was an awful noise as the back of his jeans ripped on a sharp nail.

"Oh, no!" he exclaimed.

It was Laura's turn to laugh. "I see your underwear!" she cried. "I can see your underwear!"

Now it was Zack's turn to chase
Laura. She ran up the steps and out
into the garden, where a food fight had
broken out. Pies of every flavor were
flying all over the place.

An apple pie landed splat on
Zack's chest. A cream puff hit his ear.
A stream of tomato ketchup got Mr.
Dawson on the head. Mrs. Dawson had
one foot stuck in a bucket.

Laura was wet as well. Zack had aimed a hose at her. He didn't even know he had a hose in his hand. This was so weird!

Then Zack looked at the house. It was no longer made of gingerbread. It was a real house again, but — and it was a very big BUT — one side of the house was falling over.

One whole wall was falling toward
them. It was going to crush them.
"Look out!" yelled Zack. "Look out!"

They all stopped and stared as
the wall came rushing toward them
until . . . CRASH!

Zack shut his eyes.

The wall hit the ground with a thud.

Could it be true? He was still alive. He looked around. By some amazing good luck everyone had been standing where a window frame landed.

They stood there, in the window frames, with the wall lying all around them. They looked at each other in amazement.

"Wow," said Laura, with a little smile. "That was lucky!"

"You've still got custard in your hair," Zack told her.

CHAPTER 7

BUCKETS OF BLOOD

"Can someone please tell me what's going on?" asked Mr. Dawson. "It's like some strange dream."

"More like a nightmare," said Mrs. Dawson.

"It's the cellar," Zack began.

"There isn't a cellar!" cried his father. "Stop talking about it."

"There is a cellar," said Laura.

"We've been inside it," she added. "There's a machine down there making all these things happen, and we can't get it to stop. Everything is slapstick until we change to a different story."

"What comes after slapstick?" asked Mrs. Dawson.

"That's just the problem," Zack told her. "We don't know until we push the lever."

By this time all four of them were down in the cellar. They were trying to reach the machine. They had to fight their way past piles of banana peels, flying pies, and streams of water. On top of that, everyone's pants kept falling down.

They all pushed on the lever.

CLUNK!

MURDER MYSTERY

"Oh dear," said Mrs. Dawson. "I don't like the sound of that."

There was a scream, and a dead body landed on the table beside Mrs. Dawson. There was a thud as it hit the table. Blood dripped down all over her.

The dead man had an axe stuck in his head, an arrow in his heart, and a dagger in his chest.

"Aha!" cried a stern voice from the far corner of the cellar. "You did that, Mrs. Dawson, didn't you? I am the Great Detective, and I arrest you for the murder of Lord Plummy!"

"But I didn't do it!" Mrs. Dawson told him.

"Then why is there so much blood on your hands? It's red, too, just like Lord Plummy's blood!"

"All blood is red," said Zack.

"And I arrest you, too, Zack, for helping your mother murder Lord Plummy!" cried the Great Detective.

"But, sir, they couldn't have done it," Laura told him. "They were both with me."

The Great Detective took a step back. "They were with you? Aha! Can you prove it?"

"Of course I can because I was with . . . him!" Laura pointed at Mr. Dawson. The Great Detective frowned.

"And you, sir," he said. "Where were you?"

"I was with you," Mr. Dawson told him.

"Aha! . . . I mean, what? Really? With me?" the Great Detective said, amazed. "But, but, but that would mean I DID IT! I am the murderer!"

The body on the table sat up. There was blood everywhere.

Lord Plummy gave a sigh.

"You are all useless," Lord Plummy told them. "None of you did it. The butler stabbed me. The gardener shot me with his bow and arrow, and then I stuck an axe in my head."

Lord Plummy got off the table and splashed his way to the machine.

"I'm fed up with all this murder stuff. Look what it's done to my suit. Blood everywhere! Well, it's about time to stop this nonsense." He pulled the lever.

CLUNK!

Everyone else crowded around the little window and stared at the next word.

CHAPTER 8

DON'T LOOK!

ROMANCE

That was what it said. Romance.

Zack took a quick look around the
room. His mom and dad were gone. He
was alone with Laura. The cellar was
full of sunshine. A bluebird sang in
one corner. Some butterflies flew past.
The sweet smell of roses filled the air.
He could hear a splashing waterfall.

Laura smiled at Zack.

"You're so brave," she said softly. "And good-looking."

Zack gulped. He wanted to say: Keep away from me! He wanted to say: What's going on? He wanted to yell: HELP! But he simply couldn't do it.

His mouth opened and he heard himself say, "I think you're the most beautiful girl I've ever seen."

This was an odd thing for Zack to say because by this time Laura was a mess. She still had pieces of pie all over her, as well as a lot of Lord Plummy's blood. Her face and hair were filthy.

But Zack thought Laura looked beautiful, and he told her so.

"You haven't always liked me, have you?" asked Laura, taking a step closer to Zack.

He shook his head. "You pushed me into the pool," he said.

"And you pushed me into the flower bed," she replied.

"You pushed me first," Zack said.

"I only pushed you because I liked you," said Laura. "I've always liked you," she added.

Zack couldn't move. He wasn't sure now if he wanted to run away or stay and see what would happen next.

Laura came even closer. He could hear her breathing. She held out a hand to him. She lifted her face to his.

Laura pressed up close to him, and he stepped back.

CLUNK!

He had pushed the lever. It was as if Zack woke up from a deep dream. He backed away from Laura fast. Could it be true? He was going to kiss her!

Kiss Laura?

Laura was gazing at the glass window. "It's empty," she said. "It doesn't say anything. It's over."

"Thank goodness for that," said Zack. "Come on. We have work to do."

He took Laura by the hand and pulled her up the stairs and out of the cellar. Together they pulled the cellar door shut.

Zack nailed a big board across the door. He found an old paintbrush and a can of paint. Using the brush, he added two more words to the message on the cellar door, one at the beginning and one at the end.

DEFINITELY
DON'T GO IN THE CELLAR
EVER

"That'll do it," he said.

Zack and Laura went out into the garden and fell onto the grass. They were worn out. Zack felt the warm sunshine on his face. He turned to Laura. He could see her face, but her eyes were closed.

Had she fallen asleep?

Oh well, he thought, she's okay for a girl. In fact, she's . . .

Laura's eyes were open, and she was gazing at him.

"We had a lucky escape," he said. "Who knows what might have happened?"

"Who knows what *will* happen?" said Laura as she put a hand on his arm. "Who knows?"

ABOUT THE AUTHOR

Jeremy Strong enjoys writing funny books for children. He says that he loves to make people smile and laugh. He has even had one of his books made into a TV show.

Jeremy travels throughout England and Europe talking to kids at schools and libraries. Jeremy lives in Somerset, England, United Kingdom, with his wife and cats.

GLOSSARY

cellar (SEL-ur)—a basement

cog (KOG)—one of the teeth on the edge of a wheel that turns machinery

cunning (KUHN-ing)—clever and tricky

distress (diss-TRESS)—a feeling of great pain or sadness

gleam (GLEEM)—a brief flash of light

greenhouse (GREEN-howss)—a glass building in which plants are grown

slapstick (SLAP-stik)—a type of comedy that uses horseplay and tricks

slug (SLUHG)—a slimy worm-like animal

wardrobe (WARD-robe)—a piece of furniture used to store clothes

DISCUSSION QUESTIONS

1. Zack's mother tells his father that Zack likes Laura. Why does she say this after all of the things Zack said about Laura at the beginning of the story?

2. At first, Zack's father does not believe their house has a cellar. Do you think he would change his mind if he saw the writing on Zack's bedroom wall? Why or why not?

3. Before they find the cellar, Zack doesn't want Laura to stay with them. How do you think he feels about Laura by the end of the story?

WRITING PROMPTS

1. Imagine that Zack and Laura had pushed the lever one more time, and the window said "Science Fiction." Write what would happen to Zack and Laura in a science fiction story.

2. Zack and Laura experienced many kinds of stories. What kind of story would you want to be in? Choose from horror, humor, fairy tale, mystery, or romance, and write a short story with yourself as the main character.

3. At first, Zack and Laura were afraid to go in the cellar. Write about a place you think is scary. Why does it frighten you?

INTERNET SITES

Do you want to know more about subjects related to this book? Or are you interested in learning about other topics? Then check out FactHound, a fun, easy way to find Internet sites.

Our investigative staff has already sniffed out great sites for you!

Here's how to use FactHound:

1. Visit *www.facthound.com*

2. Select your grade level.

3. To learn more about subjects related to this book, type in the book's ISBN number: **1598890026**.

4. Click the **Fetch It** button.

FactHound will fetch the best Internet sites for you!